VIVIAN DOWNS,
STARRING JODIE FOSTER

VIVIAN DOWNS,
STARRING JODIE FOSTER

A Screenplay

By Jaime Clarke

Based on his novel

VIVIAN DOWNS,
STARRING JODIE FOSTER

INT. RESTAURANT - DAY

ALEX, who bears a striking resemblance to Academy award-winning actor Jodie Foster, and her ex-wife, KAREN, sit at a table in a fancy but mostly empty Midtown Manhattan restaurant.

ALEX
I killed it. I mean, I really knew it. But the whole time they're just staring at me. You know, like always. And you know what the director says?

The WAITER approaches with their food.

WAITER
Can I get you anything else?

KAREN
We're fine.

WAITER
(to Alex)
I hope you don't mind, but I'm a fan. I loved Silence of the Lambs.

ALEX
That's kind of you. Thank you.

WAITER
I actually used to work uptown at Tupelo. I used to see you there. The bartender said you lived nearby. It just closed.

ALEX
Yes. A shame.

WAITER
I could get fired for this, but could I have your autograph? I always regretted not asking you at Tupelo.

ALEX
Sure.

The Waiter hands her a piece of paper and a pen.

WAITER
To Jared.

Alex signs it and hands it back.

KAREN
Aren't you going to tell him?

Alex gives a sheepish look.

JARED
Tell me what? I can get you anything.

Beat.

ALEX
I'm not who you think I am.

JARED
What do you mean?

KAREN
She's not the actor. She's an actor, just not Jodie Foster.

JARED
(annoyed)
That's uncool.

He crumples up the piece of paper and walks away.

ALEX
You didn't have to say anything. It's harmless.

KAREN
It's not harmless. You're proof of that.

Alex shrugs.

ALEX
I seem to remember you not minding, when we first met.

KAREN
At Mary Cotton's party? That was a thousand years ago.

ALEX
But you thought I was her.

KAREN
Maybe for a minute.

ALEX
(teasing)
Was more than a minute.

Karen smiles.

ALEX (CONT'D)
Did you see her next movie?

KAREN
How would I know her next movie? I'm not obsessed with her.

ALEX
Let's not...Let's just have a nice lunch.

Karen puts up her hands, surrender-style.

ALEX (CONT'D)
She's playing Vivian Downs.

KAREN
How are they making a movie about a writer? Sounds boring.

ALEX
Remember that piece in the Times that said Downs walks around New York just living her life under everyone's noses?

KAREN
No.

ALEX
It's based on that, I think.

KAREN
I've never understood why you like her books so much. The Jodie Foster thing I get. But those books are pretentious.

ALEX
God, I would be perfect for that role. I'm actually a fan. Jodie Foster's not even a fan.

KAREN
How do you know?

ALEX
Never heard her mention Downs in an interview.

KAREN
I wish you'd been half as obsessed about me when we were married. You know the kinds of books Jodie Foster likes, but I'll bet you don't know what books I like.

ALEX
That's not fair. You don't read.

KAREN
My favorite movie, then.

ALEX
You liked Contact. Little Man Tate maybe?

KAREN
(impatiently)
My favorite non-Jodie Foster movie.

Alex thinks.

KAREN (CONT'D)
Doesn't matter.

ALEX
C'mon. Let's just have a nice lunch.

KAREN
Tell me what the director said.

ALEX
You won't believe it. I'm in the middle of the audition, I
know it backward and forward and the director stops me and
says—not to me but to the casting director—"If I wanted
Jodie Foster, I'd get Jodie Foster." I mean, what is that?

Karen looks at her, considering.

KAREN
Fuck it. We're not married anymore so I'll just say it: You
have to forget acting. I know it's not fair, but this happens
every god damn time. It used to kill me to see how it would
devastate you, but at some point you just doubled down. It's

like the more movies Jodie Foster makes, and the more
awards she wins, the more auditions you go on, as if to
prove...to prove what?

ALEX
(angrily)
That's crazy. Not true.

KAREN
If only you'd doubled down on us. Who knows?

ALEX
Don't do this. I need your support. No one else understands.
I've got an audition uptown tomorrow and I can't hear this.

Karen stands to leave.

KAREN
I told you this when we decided to call it quits: I still love
you, but this...thing...is mental. And you know it. And if you
don't know it, it's worse than I thought. And don't call me
every time you need fluffed for an audition.

ALEX
C'mon, sit down.

KAREN
I just can't anymore.

She leaves. Jared, who has been waiting, brings the check
immediately and sets it down unceremoniously.

EXT. MANHATTAN STREET - DAY

A DOORMAN holds the door for ALEX, who comes out of
an Upper West Side apartment building looking distraught.
She crumples a few script pages and tosses them into the

nearest trash can and starts walking.

EXT. MANHATTAN STREET - CONTINUOUS

Alex stops on a corner for a red light. She spies the newsstand and saunters over.

NEWSAGENT
I thought you'd left already.

A MAN steps between them and buys a paper, giving Alex a moment to think.

NEWSAGENT (CONT'D)
Change your mind?

Alex shrugs and smiles, unsure of how to respond. The Newsagent slaps a pack of Big Red gum on the counter.

NEWSAGENT (CONT'D)
The usual?

ALEX
Changed my mind, yeah.

Alex pays for the gum and pockets it.

WOMAN (O.S.)
Do you have the new VANITY FAIR?

Alex moves out of the way and the WOMAN approaches the counter. Alex crosses the street and continues on her way.

EXT. MANHATTAN STREET - CONTINUOUS

Alex is walking when a MAN and a WOMAN call out.

MAN
Excuse me!

WOMAN
Is it really?

FACES on the street turn to look at the commotion but keep
moving.

ALEX
I'm sorry, but—

MAN
Could we have your autograph?

WOMAN
We're huge fans.

ALEX
That's nice of you, really.

The WOMAN holds out a random scrap of paper and a pen.
Alex takes it and signs it. The MAN takes a picture without
asking.

WOMAN
I can't believe it.

She looks at the autograph to remember her name.

WOMAN (CONT'D)
Jodie Foster, right. Wow.

MAN
She's too embarrassed to tell you, but she cried at the end of
Contact.

The Woman hits the Man playfully.

ALEX
No need to be embarrassed.

WOMAN
My father loves the Maverick remake.

MAN
We love it too.

WOMAN
Right, true. True.

Alex smiles and nods and makes to go.

WOMAN (CONT'D)
Thank you for stopping. I just had a feeling you'd be real.
We met this other famous actor at a friend's wedding, and
Tom happened to be using the restroom same time as this
actor—

TOM
She doesn't want to hear this story.

Alex smiles as if to say it's okay.

WOMAN
And Tom tells him how much he likes this actor's movies,
and the actor, this prick—excuse me—says, "I don't meet
people in the men's room."

TOM
He wasn't a prick.

Alex is amused by the story but wants to get away. In the

background a DOORMAN can be seen watching the whole exchange.

WOMAN
(gasps)
Oh, I forgot you were in that one movie together! I'm sorry.

TOM
Forget she said anything.
(to Woman)
Let's go. I'm hungry.

WOMAN
I'm so sorry. Thank you again.

Alex smiles as Tom and the Woman walk away. The Woman is fretting inaudibly.

TOM (O.S.)
You never said the name of the movie.

Alex takes a few steps forward, and the DOORMAN, who has been hovering in the background, opens the door to the building.

DOORMAN
Everything okay, Ms. Foster?

Alex stops, confused.

DOORMAN (CONT'D)
We had a note that you'd left.

INT. BUILDING LOBBY - CONTINUOUS

Alex steps inside, the Doorman following.

DOORMAN
Let me get your mail.

The Doorman goes behind the desk and retrieves a bundle of mail and hands it to Alex. Alex sees the mail addressed to Jodie Foster at the building's address, including the apartment number.

DOORMAN (CONT'D)
I'll leave a note about the mistake, Ms. Foster. Very sorry about that.

ALEX
It's no problem, really. Crossed wires. It happens.

DOORMAN
Thanks for understanding.

Alex nods and walks through the lobby to the bank of elevators, stops, and turns back.

ALEX
My keys...

DOORMAN
Ah. Left them upstairs again?

ALEX
Exactly.

DOORMAN
Give me a minute.

INT. ELEVATOR - MOMENTS LATER

Alex looks at herself in the mirror inside the elevator, scrutinizing. She's wondering if she's going to go through with it. She looks at the mail she's holding, including a copy of the latest issue of a trade magazine. She instinctively turns to the audition listings and scans them. The elevator DINGS and the doors open.

INT. HALLWAY - CONTINUOUS

Alex looks at the mail again to check the apartment number. She locates the correct door and inserts the key.

INT. JODIE FOSTER'S APARTMENT - CONTINUOUS

Alex surveys the landscape. Takes in the modestly but tastefully decorated apartment. The phone RINGS, startling her. The answering machine picks up on the second ring.

JODIE FOSTER'S RECORDED VOICE
Sorry I missed you. Leave a message and I'll return your call.

There's a loud BEEP and then a CLICK when no message is left.

Alex is drawn to the answering machine, which shows two unheard messages. She presses the button on the answering to listen to the messages.

AUTOMATED VOICE
Message one.

MEL GIBSON
Jodie, I hope you haven't left yet. We have to talk about Matt. I'm worried about him. Call me.

AUTOMATED VOICE
Message two.

MALE VOICE
It's Barry. I know you're gone and that you're incommunicado but wanted you to know that I reached out to Downs through a backchannel—really had to call in a favor—but she said she wouldn't see you. So that's that. Call me when you're back.

A LOUD DIAL TONE plays, and Alex presses the button on the answering machine to stop it, but it doesn't. She lifts the receiver just as it gives a HALF RING.

WOMAN'S VOICE (O.S.)
Hello?

Alex presses the receiver against her ear.

ALEX
Yes?

WOMAN'S VOICE (O.S.)
Is this Miss Foster?

Alex appears nervous.

ALEX
Yes?

WOMAN'S VOICE (O.S.)
This is Vivian Downs.

ALEX
(surprised)
Oh. Yes.

DOWNS (O.S.)
I heard you want to speak with me.

ALEX
I would——. It would be an honor.

DOWNS (O.S.)
I haven't even seen the script for this thing. Do I want to?

ALEX
(panicked)
Probably not. I mean, it's very good, but I imagine it's hard to, um, read about yourself.

Alex grimaces during the silence that follows.

DOWNS (O.S.)
Hmm. Well, I can always sue, right?

ALEX
Can I just say how much of a fan I am? I really——. It's the role of my career.

DOWNS (O.S.)
Yes, yes, okay. Well, how about coming over tomorrow and we can talk. 425 Madison.

ALEX
It would be a pleasure

DOWNS (O.S.)
See you at ten.

Downs hangs up. Alex replaces the receiver. She spots a matchbook bearing the name of the bar Maxwell Jay's in a change dish.

INT. MAXWELL JAY'S - NIGHT

Alex enters and the BARTENDER gives a knowing nod. The

Bartender pours a Maker's Mark neat and sets it at the corner stool. Alex sits in front of it.

BARTENDER
Nice to see you.

Alex lifts her glass in salute.

BARTENDER (CONT'D)
She was in here the other night looking for you. Like you thought. I told her you were gone, like you said.

ALEX
Thanks.

A MAN in his late fifties waves down the Bartender. The Man nods at Alex, as if in recognition. Alex nods back. The Bartender sets the Man's drink in front of him and moves on to another customer.

MAN
I'm sorry to bother you, but you're Jodie Foster, right?

ALEX
What's your name?

The Man moves a few seats closer.

MAN
Burton. Burton LaFarge.

ALEX
Nice to meet you, Burton

BURTON
I can't believe it. I've lived here ten years and have never seen a celebrity. Amazing.

Alex smiles.

ALEX
What do you do, Burton?

BURTON
I'm a writer. Unpublished so far.

ALEX
Just takes a lucky break.

BURTON
That's what I keep hoping for. At my age, though, who knows?

ALEX
What do you write?

BURTON
Novels, mostly. Dabble a little in screenplays. Had a play produced off-Broadway.

ALEX
Congratulations.

The Bartender comes over.

BARTENDER
Excuse me, Jodie. You have a call.

Alex looks at the Bartender, confused. But then realizes it's a ruse Jodie Foster and the Bartender have worked out in case she needs bailed out.

BARTENDER (CONT'D)
Should I take a message?

ALEX
Yes, please.

The Bartender leaves.

BURTON
I take it this is your regular.

ALEX
It's a nice place.

Beat.

BURTON
This might seem crazy, but maybe your being here is a lucky
break.

Alex looks at him.

ALEX
I've never been anyone's lucky charm.

Burton moves over until he's sitting next to Alex.

BURTON
I came here tonight to celebrate finishing a new script. I
never think about casting when writing. That kills it. But
seeing you here. You'd be perfect.

ALEX
I can only read scripts sent to me by my agent, sorry.

BURTON
Oh, you don't have to worry about all of that. I'm not a kook.
I'm covered if someone lifts my idea, though maybe you'll
agree that only a low-life no-talent would steal someone
else's ideas.

Pulls the script from his bag before Alex can protest further. The script sits between them on the bar.

BURTON (CONT'D)
Even if you aren't interested, I'd love your opinion.

An awkward beat passes between them.

ALEX
Okay.

BURTON
(beaming)
Terrific. This is me.

Scribbles his phone number on the cover of the script.

BURTON (CONT'D)
Who knows? Maybe a great movie was made because two people met in a bar.

Gathers hurriedly to go in case Alex changes her mind.

ALEX
(shrugs)
Anything's possible.

Picks up the script and waves it at Burton.

BURTON
Today I'm a believer.

Waves as he leaves.

BARTENDER
Everything ok?

Alex nods and fans the script without reading any of it.

EXT. MAXWELL JAY'S - LATER

Alex exits, depositing the script in the nearest trash can.

INT. JODIE FOSTER'S APARTMENT - NIGHT

Alex lies on the couch, asleep, one of Vivian Downs's novels open on her chest.

EXT. 425 MADISON AVENUE - DAY

Alex BUZZES an apartment. No answer. She BUZZES again, and as she does, a WOMAN IN HER THIRTIES exits.

ALEX
Hold the door?

The Woman is about to object, but a look of recognition comes over her face.

WOMAN
You're here to see my mother.

Alex nods.

WOMAN (CONT'D)
Veronica Downs. I'm a fan.

ALEX
Nice of you.

VERONICA
I'm so glad my mother changed her mind. She never does that.

ALEX
Did you have a hand in that?

VERONICA
(matter-of-factly)
My mother has never been under anyone's influence, family
included.

Alex looks up, taking in the building.

VERONICA (CONT'D)
She used to live in a nicer building. But, you know, the thing
with the doorman.

Alex nods as if she understands.

VERONICA (CONT'D)
She's on the top floor.

Steps aside so Alex can pass.

ALEX
Thank you. I'll see you again, hopefully.

VERONICA
That depends on what happens in the next hour or so,
guessing.

She smiles and waves good-bye.

INT. 425 MADISON AVENUE - CONTINUOUS

Alex enters the foyer and mounts the stairs.

INT. 425 MADISON AVENUE - MOMENTS LATER

Alex KNOCKS on Downs's door.

WOMAN'S VOICE (O.S.)
Yes, come in.

Alex enters the apartment, a cluttered warren. From an unseen hallway, VIVIAN DOWNS appears and gives a cautious look. She and Alex stand looking at each other for a moment, as if they're both staring in the mirror, save for the fact that Downs wears glasses.

ALEX
(nervously)
It's an honor, ma'am.

DOWNS
Let's skip all of that. Would you like some tea?

INT. VIVIAN DOWNS'S APARTMENT - MOMENTS LATER

Alex and Downs are sitting in the living room, facing each other in high-backed chairs, drinking tea.

ALEX
I just met your daughter.

DOWNS
She checks on me more often than she need.

ALEX
Nice of her.

DOWNS
It's a source of sadness for me, actually. Somewhere along the line she bought into the myth about me being a lonely recluse.

Sips her tea.

DOWNS (CONT'D)
But I get along as well as anyone else. More or less.

ALEX
It's said that people don't recognize you when you go out.

DOWNS
You'd be surprised by what people don't see.

ALEX
If they're not looking, you mean.

DOWNS
A low profile is better than no profile. Salinger made a mistake when he disappeared. It made everyone hunt him.

Alex nods.

DOWNS (CONT'D)
I imagine the same is true for actors. A little curiosity is fine, but you have to be careful not to create a mystery that people wish to solve.

ALEX
That's it, yes.

DOWNS
I agreed to see you to impress upon you just that point. If I could stop this movie from being made, I would. My contempt for Hollywood is immeasurable. But I'm advised otherwise. So if it's going to go forward, my request is that it doesn't make my life harder than need be.

ALEX
Absolutely.

DOWNS
I hate the movies. It's your profession, I know, but I want to be up front about my feelings.

ALEX
I appreciate that.

DOWNS
Films are needless purveyors of phoniness. There are very few truths to be found in the movies.

ALEX
Some people just like to escape.

DOWNS
(amused)
Ah, yes. Not everything is in service of the truth, as I'm constantly reminded.
(beat)
I didn't appreciate your representative reaching out to me through my friend. I purposely left his letter unanswered.

ALEX
I'm sorry about that.

DOWNS
Why is this meeting necessary? I'm being made an accomplice in my own debasing.

ALEX
(forgetting herself for a moment)
I'm sure they just want to be as accurate as possible.

DOWNS
I was under the impression you wanted this meeting.

ALEX
(remembering her role)
Oh, yes. It's just—. Well, it's an enormous responsibility to portray a real person. Especially someone like yourself.

DOWNS
It's an impersonation, not a portrayal.

Alex lets the comment pass.

DOWNS (CONT'D)
I was surprised that you were interested in this role.

ALEX
Oh?

DOWNS
I know you're a serious actor, not one of those new actors who are hired to stand and project their looks into the camera.

ALEX
I'm a fan of your work and wanted to do you justice.

DOWNS
I'm not sure I deserve justice, or want it.

ALEX
I'd think anyone would.

DOWNS
Would it offend you if I used your alleged appreciation for my books against you and ask you not to make this movie?

ALEX
Is that why you agreed to see me?

Downs tilts her head.

ALEX (CONT'D)
They'll just get someone else. There's always someone else.

DOWNS
I suppose you're right.

Awkward beat.

ALEX
Is there anything that would make you feel better about my taking the role?

DOWNS
I'm under the impression that my consent isn't necessary.

ALEX
For me, then.

Downs considers.

DOWNS
Part of the phoniness of the movies is that they give the appearance of sustained storytelling, but in truth they're filmed seconds and minutes at a time over the course of months.

Alex nods.

DOWNS (CONT'D)
That reduces your...impression...of me to a series of bits, as if I were some kind of nightclub act.

ALEX
The medium dictates that, yes.

Beat.

DOWNS
What if you had to become me for not seconds or minutes but hours and days? I've heard some actors inhabit their characters in this way.

ALEX
Yes.

DOWNS
You have a reputation for such a method.

ALEX
(smiling)
I abhor all manner of flattery.

Downs likes this response.

DOWNS
This is what I propose: I'm traveling to Florida to avoid the press surrounding the publication of my new book. The last go-round was a nightmare. While I'm gone, you'll be my doppelganger here in the city. I'll give you the details of my upcoming social obligations, and we'll see if you can fool everyone into believing that you are me. If you can do that, I'll give my blessing to the film by not causing a legal ruckus over it.

Alex is blown away by this offer.

ALEX
What happens if I'm found out?

DOWNS
My lawyer has already drafted a cease and desist letter for the film's producers.

Alex considers this.

ALEX
Will I be able to reach you if I need to?

DOWNS
Where I'm going, no one can reach me.

Alex gets a confident look on his face.

DOWNS (CONT'D)
What do you say? Want to put your acting skills to the challenge?

INT. JODIE FOSTER'S APARTMENT – LATER

Alex presses the button on the answering machine and listens to the messages as she takes off her coat and kicks off her shoes.

AUTOMATED VOICE
Message one.

MEL GIBSON (O.S.)
Jodie, it's Mel again. Hoping to catch you before you leave. Matt's not returning my calls. It might be up to you.

AUTOMATED VOICE
Message two.

DENZEL WASHINGTON (O.S.)
Yeah, it's Denzel. I'll be in New York at the end of the month. Would love to see you.

AUTOMATED VOICE
Message three.

ETHAN HAWKE (O.S.)
Jodie? Pick up. It's Ethan.
(beat)
I guess you're not home. It's Matt. He won't listen to anyone
but you. Give me a call.

As the last message ends, a WOMAN IN HER THIRTIES
enters, a look of surprise on her face. Alex also gives a
startled look.

WOMAN
I didn't know you'd still be here.

Alex remains startled, unsure if she's caught.

WOMAN (CONT'D)
What happened?

ALEX
What do you mean?

WOMAN
Your plans. Weren't you supposed to fly out yesterday?

ALEX
Changed my mind.

WOMAN
(cautiously hopeful)
About everything?

Alex shrugs. She doesn't really know what the Woman is
talking about and wants to change the subject.

WOMAN (CONT'D)
Should I come back later?

Alex hesitates. Wants the company.

ALEX
Stay for a drink?

WOMAN
I could do with a glass of wine.

Alex moves to the kitchen and the Woman follows. Alex removes two wineglasses from the cupboard, reaches for a bottle of red, and pours a glass each. Woman looks at him askance.

WOMAN (CONT'D)
White for me, please.

Alex pretends to remember.

ALEX
Oh, right. Sorry.

She finds a bottle of white in the fridge and pours it under the Woman's watchful eye. Alex holds up her glass and they CLINK them together and drink.

WOMAN
You're in a better mood. What are we toasting?

ALEX
You'll never guess who I just met with.

WOMAN
You're right.

ALEX
Vivian Downs.

Woman raises her eyebrows.

WOMAN
Wow.

ALEX
I'm such a fan of her work.

Woman gives her a look.

WOMAN
Is that for the audience?

ALEX
What?

WOMAN
You said her books were trash when they offered you the part.

Sensing something, Alex backs off.

ALEX
(mildly)
She has a couple of good books.

Woman eyes her a little more.

WOMAN
Did she mention the resemblance?

ALEX
No. But I think she likes the casting.

WOMAN
Did she say that?

Alex takes her wine and moves into the front room. Woman follows.

ALEX
She wants me to impersonate her with her friends and colleagues while she's away, to see if I can fool them. Like an audition.

Woman is intrigued.

WOMAN
Is she crazy?

ALEX
Who knows. Maybe.

WOMAN
What did you tell her?

Alex smiles.

WOMAN (CONT'D)
You might be crazy too.

ALEX
It is a good test.

WOMAN
A movie is one thing. This is this person's life. Why doesn't she just invite a friend over and have you answer the door if she wants to test you?

ALEX
I'm up to the challenge.

Sips her wine.

WOMAN
(playfully)
You who have nothing left to prove.

She gets up and disappears into the bathroom. Alex waits to hear the DOOR CLICK and sets her wineglass down. She reaches for the Woman's purse and pulls out her wallet, searching for her driver's license to learn her name: Jessica Oliver.

INT. JODIE FOSTER'S APARTMENT - HALLWAY - CONTINUOUS

Jessica is watching Alex look at her license from the bathroom door. She COUGHS and Alex scrambles to put the license back.

INT. JODIE FOSTER'S APARTMENT - CONTINUOUS

Alex takes up her wineglass and Jessica re-enters.

ALEX
You can't say anything.

JESSICA
Who am I going to tell?

ALEX
A girlfriend, co-worker, whatever. Anyone knows and it'll end up in the papers.

Jessica sits down next to her on the couch, close. She stares into Alex's face with a searching look. Smiles.

JESSICA
Speaking of co-workers, don't forget the fund-raiser tomorrow night.

ALEX
Fund-raiser?

JESSICA
Not even funny. You're the main attraction. You promised.

INT. RESTAURANT - NIGHT

Crowded restaurant. Well-dressed people are mingling.
Poster on an easel by the door announces fund-raiser for the
cure for breast cancer, with an appearance by Jodie Foster.
A KNOT OF PEOPLE surround Alex, with Jessica at her
side. Alex autographs a program for the evening's festivities,
smiling. She takes pictures with people who have cameras.

INT. RESTAURANT - WOMEN'S ROOM - A LITTLE
LATER

Alex is washing her hands and studying herself in the mirror.

FEMALE VOICE #1 (O.S.)
She said she changed her mind.

FEMALE VOICE #2 (O.S.)
Wonder how she got her to change it.

FEMALE VOICE #1 (O.S.)
Maybe she brought her dog back.

Alex gives a final look in the mirror, as if readying herself to
rejoin the fray.

FEMALE VOICE #2 (O.S.)
Do you think she really took the dog?

FEMALE VOICE #1 (O.S.)
She admitted it to her assistant.

FEMALE VOICE #2 (O.S.)
The flyers are still up around the neighborhood.

Alex walks out of the women's room and finds Jessica
waiting for her.

JESSICA
You okay?

ALEX
Ready for more.

Jessica smiles.

A WOMAN IN HER SIXTIES approaches with a wide
smile.

JESSICA
(to Alex)
Jodie, this is my boss, Emily St. Cloud.

Alex extends a hand.

ALEX
It's a pleasure.

EMILY ST. CLOUD
(beaming)
I'm such a fan.

ALEX
(shyly)
That's very kind of you.

EMILY ST. CLOUD
I just wanted to personally thank you for this wonderful
evening.

ALEX
Always happy to help a good cause.

VOICE (O.S.)
Jodie, can I take a picture with you?

ALEX
Excuse me.

Turns away from Emily and Jessica.

EMILY ST. CLOUD
(to Jessica, coldly)
Congratulations. You get to keep your job.

INT. CAB - THAT NIGHT

Alex and Jessica are in the backseat as the cab moves
through traffic.

JESSICA
Thank you for doing that.

Alex gives her a look that says she's a little intoxicated by
the rush from so much adoration. She reaches over and puts
her hand on Jessica's. Jessica gives her a look she doesn't
see, realizing a problem she didn't think through.

INT. JODIE FOSTER'S APARTMENT - THAT NIGHT

Alex and Jessica enter. As Alex takes off her coat and
unwinds, Jessica walks straight to the guest room.

JESSICA
Good night.

ALEX
Good night?

JESSICA
Early start tomorrow.

Alex furrows her brow.

JESSICA (CONT'D)
And I think I'm coming down with something. I'm gonna crash in the guest room.

Alex gives her a long look.

ALEX
Feel better.

Jessica gives a wan smile and disappears into the guest room. Alex leans back on the couch, looking around, satisfied. Feeling self-congratulatory.

INT. PUBLISHING OFFICE - DAY

Alex saunters through the bull pen of cubicles, glasses on, moving toward a glass corner office. ASSISTANTS glance up from their work as she passes, and there's a MURMUR. Vivian Downs sightings are few and far between. She reaches the office, the name Barbara West stenciled on the door. BARBARA, an impeccably dressed elegant woman in her 60s, moves from around the desk to greet her at the door.

INT. BARBARA'S OFFICE - CONTINUOUS

Barbara extends her hand and Alex shakes it.

BARBARA
I'm so glad to see you again. It's been too long.

Alex winces as she imagines Vivian would.

BARBARA (CONT'D)
Please.

She indicates the chair in front of the desk. Alex sits down.
Barbara closes the door and retakes her seat behind her desk.
She reaches next to her and produces a copy of Downs's new
book. She hands it to Alex.

BARBARA (CONT'D)
It arrived from the printer this morning.

Alex takes the book and turns it over in her hands. She's
struggling to contain her enthusiasm at being among the first
to have a copy of Downs's new book, but also maintaining
her indifference to being impressed, as Downs would.

BARBARA (CONT'D)
Your cover came out beautifully. As I knew it would.

Alex sets the book down on the desk.

ALEX
Yes.

BARBARA
And I know you don't care to know anything about reviews,
but you'll be on the cover of the Sunday Times Book
Review, naturally.

Alex nods.

BARBARA (CONT'D)
Before I tell you why I asked you to come in, let me preface
this by saying that those above me are behind the maneuver. I
explained to them your resistance to requests like these and

even tried to turn it down on your behalf, as I always do. If Barry knew how many requests I don't pass along, he'd have no choice but to make me your co-agent and give me a percentage.

Alex tries to hide her anxiety. She picks up the book, looks at it, and sets it back down.

ALEX
Okay.

BARBARA
It's so outlandish a proposition that I can't believe I'm repeating it, but I'm being asked to ask you if you would make an appearance on the Charlie Austin show.

A silence falls between them and Barbara shifts in her seat.

ALEX
I can't remember the last time I was on television.

BARBARA
(gives a look)
You've never been on television.

Alex squirms uncomfortably.

ALEX
Exactly.

BARBARA
I know it's ridiculous, and the book certainly doesn't need the push, but it would mean something to the owners of the publishing house.

ALEX
Why should I care?

BARBARA
(conspiratorially)
You shouldn't.

ALEX
What will happen to you if I decline?

Barbara shrugs, though with trepidation.

BARBARA
The only reason I agreed to ask you is that I wondered if you might want the opportunity to be on the record. For posterity, I mean.

ALEX
Posterity?

BARBARA
Or for future readers of your work.

Alex gives a look that indicates she doesn't care about what Barbara is saying.

BARBARA (CONT'D)
Or maybe as some truth serum to whatever this movie is going to say about you.
(beat)
I saw they got Jodie Foster to play you.

ALEX
I met with her the other day.

BARBARA
(surprised)
Oh?

ALEX
I agreed to see her to impress upon her my concerns about making my life more miserable than it is in terms of fans. And to tell her about my immeasurable contempt for Hollywood.

BARBARA
How did she take that?

ALEX
She didn't like it. But I think my message got through. Films are needless purveyors of phoniness. There are very few truths to be found in movies.

BARBARA
You were wise not to give consent. I'm sure the movie will be inaccurate however it comes out.
(beat)
She's a fine actor, though.

ALEX
The idea of them making such a film is preposterous.

BARBARA
Agreed.

Awkward pause.

BARBARA (CONT'D)
In your last letter you mentioned a problem with your daughter's husband. Did that get resolved?

Alex doesn't know what she's referring to.

ALEX
Yes.

BARBARA
Thank goodness. Was she more annoyed or frightened when he disappeared like that?

ALEX
She never tells me anything. I was annoyed, though.

BARBARA
I can imagine. Publishing is full of similarly unreliable characters.
(laughs)
Speaking of characters. The mailbags are full of the usual crazy letters for you, which we'll continue to shred unless we hear otherwise—

Alex indicates it's okay to keep shredding them.

BARBARA (CONT'D)
And as I mentioned on the phone, lately we've been getting some packages messengered over from someone making outrageous claims.

She holds up the new novel.

BARBARA (CONT'D)
He's very persistent. To the point that I've alerted building security. There's some concern that he's delivering the packages himself. Would you like to see them?

Alex shakes her head no.

BARBARA (CONT'D)
I'm sure he'll go away like all the other pests over the years. I'll dispose of whatever he sends.

ALEX
So many nuts.

Alex stands to leave. She picks up the copy of the novel. Barbara realizes it's the abrupt end of the meeting and stands too.

BARBARA
If you ever need anything from me, just ask.

ALEX
I appreciate that.

An awkward silence passes between them.

BARBARA
What shall I tell the gentlemen upstairs? They're expecting me to deliver your answer.

ALEX
I'm sure they are.

BARBARA
If I had to bet, I'd say they'll call me before you even leave the building.

ALEX
I'm sorry this is around your neck, but—

Barbara winces, bracing for the answer. Alex looks at her sympathetically.

ALEX (CONT'D)
Why not? At the very least, perhaps the movie people will see it and adjust their portrayal accordingly.

Barbara smiles, relieved.

INT. MAXWELL JAY'S - NIGHT

Alex is sitting at the bar over a Maker's Mark neat. The Bartender is nearby, washing glasses.

ALEX
Nah, we're back together.

The Bartender gives a nod. Alex takes a sip of her drink.

BARTENDER
I'll put her back on the call list.

Alex smiles.

Burton LaFarge saunters in and takes an empty stool a few stools down. Alex glances at him and there's a flicker of recognition, but she's having a hard time placing him. Burton waves and Alex nods.

BURTON
(pointing at himself)
Burton.

ALEX
(remembering)
Yes. How are you?

BURTON
Another day in the big city of small dreams.

Alex laughs.

BARTENDER
(to Burton)
What'll it be?

Burton gives the Bartender a look. He doesn't appreciate the Bartender's aggressiveness.

BURTON
You got Black Pony scotch?

Bartender gives him a skeptical look.

BARTENDER
Never heard of it.

BURTON
(to Alex)
He's never heard of Black Pony scotch.

Alex takes a laconic sip of her drink. Doesn't want to get involved in the conversation.

BURTON (CONT'D)
It was called Four Horses in the stage version.

BARTENDER
Stage version of what?

BURTON
(to Alex)
Believe this guy?

Alex doesn't react.

BURTON (CONT'D)
The movie Laura. One of the classics.

Looks at Alex conspiratorially. The Bartender pours a beer and sets it on the bar.

BARTENDER
This or nothing.

BURTON
Okay, okay. Jeez.

Puts some money on the bar and takes the beer. He raises his glass in Alex's direction. Alex gives a small salute in return.

BURTON (CONT'D)
Dying to know what you thought of it.

ALEX
Of what?

BURTON
(disappointed)
My screenplay.

Alex remembers Burton now.

ALEX
I get a lot of screenplays. Haven't had a chance to read it yet.

BURTON
(crestfallen)
Oh.

Beat. Alex signals to the Bartender for another drink.

BURTON (CONT'D)
It's just...the other night when we met, it seemed like it was destiny.

The Bartender looks at Alex, who raises her eyebrows and sips his drink. A COUPLE comes in and sits at the other end of the bar, and the Bartender moves over to them, out of earshot.

ALEX
What did Shakespeare say about destiny?

BURTON
"It is not in the stars to hold our destiny but in ourselves."

ALEX
Sounds right.

BURTON
(emphatically)
Yes. Yes, exactly.

Moves closer to Alex.

BURTON (CONT'D)
This is me holding my own destiny.

Reaches into his bag and produces the stained copy of the screenplay he wrote his phone number on. Alex realizes Burton retrieved it from the garbage can. Burton hands it back to Alex, finishes his beer in a long draft, and stands to leave.

BURTON (CONT'D)
Really would love to hear what you think.

INT. DINER - DAY

Alex enters. She's wearing glasses to resemble Vivian Downs. She catches the eye of the WAITRESS, a woman in her 50s, who nods at a booth in the corner. Alex sits in the booth and opens the menu. As the Waitress nears, Alex sees the name badge pinned to her shirt: DEANNA.

DEANNA
Facing out today. That's new.

Alex looks at her quizzically.

DEANNA (CONT'D)
Thought you liked your back to the door.

ALEX
Trying something new.

DEANNA
And I assume the open menu means you're having something other than your usual?

Alex closes the menu too quickly.

ALEX
The usual is fine, Deanna.

Deanna gives her a second look and then turns for the kitchen. Alex looks out the window. A GIRL IN HER TWENTIES in a far booth catches her eye and smiles. She holds up a copy of one of Vivian Downs's books and points at the cover, and Alex smiles and nods, which the Girl takes as an invitation to approach.

GIRL
This is one of the most remarkable things that has ever happened to me.

ALEX
Well, you're young yet.

GIRL
I'm Callie. Huge fan.

Awkward beat where Callie wonders if Alex is going to ask
her to sit down.

ALEX
Would you like me to sign your book?

CALLIE
Would you?

She uses the invitation to sit across from Alex.

ALEX
Happy to.

Callie slides the book across the table. Alex opens to the
bookmarked page.

ALEX (CONT'D)
Page thirty-three?

CALLIE
I'm rereading it!

Alex smiles. Her pen hovers over the title page as she
realizes she doesn't know how to sign Vivian Downs's name.
She draws a smiley face and writes You Just Met Vivian
Downs and makes a squiggly line. She passes the book back
to Callie as Deanna approaches the table with black coffee
and a plate of scrambled eggs and dry toast. She furrows her
brow at the sight of Callie.

DEANNA
(to Callie)
Please don't bother our customers, sweetheart.

CALLIE
I was invited.

Deanna verifies this with Alex with a look.

ALEX
It's okay.

DEANNA
Opposite day, huh?

She walks away but doesn't go far. She gives Alex a look that spooks her.

CALLIE
Mind if I ask you a question?

ALEX
Shoot.

CALLIE
Do people tell you that you look like Jodie Foster?

Alex shrugs.

CALLIE (CONT'D)
I wonder if people tell her that she looks like you.

ALEX
She's a great actor.

Deanna overhears this and is curious.

ALEX (CONT'D)
Know which movies she won Oscars for?

CALLIE
Easy. Silence of the Lambs and Nell.

ALEX
(smiling)
That's what everyone thinks.
(beat)
Silence of the Lambs and The Accused.

CALLIE
Oh she was scary good in The Accused.

Alex nods, sips her coffee.

CALLIE (CONT'D)
Huh.

Deanna appears and refills Alex's coffee without asking.

DEANNA
(to Callie)
I left your check, honey.

Walks away.

CALLIE
(checks her watch)
Whoa. I'm late.

ALEX
School?

CALLIE
Job interview.

ALEX
Good luck.

CALLIE
(joking)
Can I use you as a reference?

Alex smiles as Callie stands.

CALLIE (CONT'D)
Thanks for talking to me. I won't tell anyone you eat here.

Callie walks back to her booth, leaves cash for the check, and walks out with her stuff.

Deanna comes to Alex's table.

DEANNA
Since when are you such a movie buff?

Alex looks at her a little fearfully as she makes up the check and puts it on the table.

DEANNA (CONT'D)
Stay as long as you'd like.
(beat)
Whoever you are.

Alex stares at the check until Deanna walks away.

EXT. BROOKLYN WAREHOUSE - NIGHT

Marquee advertises Gotham Dance Company performance: Twilight

INT. BROOKLYN WAREHOUSE - CONTINUOUS

Alex and Jessica are sitting in the front row of some risers set up inside the warehouse. Throughout the scene the people behind them intermittently look over at Alex, mistaking her for Jodie Foster.

VOICE (O.S.)
(low)
God, I loved Anna and the King.

JESSICA
I'm sure it was just waitress talk.

ALEX
(worried)
I think she knew.

JESSICA
There's no way she could know.

ALEX
Think about it. She probably spends more time with Downs than anyone else. And I'm supposed to go to this dinner party with her friends. Maybe I shouldn't.

A DANCER, A WOMAN IN HER THIRTIES, walks over. Jessica stands and hugs her.

DANCER
Thank you for coming!

JESSICA
Of course.
(to Alex)
You remember Chase.

Alex stands. Several heads turn in her direction as she does.

ALEX
Yes, hello.

CHASE
(implying a double meaning)
This makes me happy.

JESSICA
We still on for drinks after?

CHASE
Definitely.

INT. BAR - LATER THAT NIGHT
Alex and Jessica are standing at a small table near the bar.
Bar patrons glance at Alex, mistaking her for Jodie Foster.
Chase cuts through the crowd with a COUPLE OF OTHER
WOMEN IN THEIR THIRTIES in tow. All smile when they
see Alex.

JESSICA
(to Chase)
You were terrific.

CHASE
Thanks, doll.

The two Women with Chase take positions at the table and
Jessica rushes their introductions before they can speak.

JESSICA
(to Alex)
You remember Margot and Nina.

ALEX
Of course.

MARGOT
I was flipping through the channels the other night and The
Courtship of Eddie's Father was on.

Alex smiles but doesn't say anything.

MARGOT (CONT'D)
You were so good even back then.

Chase and Jessica have a side conversation:

CHASE
When did this happen?

JESSICA
A couple of days ago.

CHASE
I'm so glad.

While this conversation goes on in the background:

MARGOT
That show was on for years.

NINA
I wish it was still on.

Alex shrugs sheepishly. She looks away, toward the bar, and glimpses Burton LaFarge, who waves. Alex pretends not to see him.

CHASE
Jessica says you're playing Vivian Downs.

ALEX
Yes.

NINA
Didn't she write that book about the yuppie serial killer?

ALEX
Among others.

MARGOT
The movie of that book was terrible.

JESSICA
I thought it was better than the book.

MARGOT
I didn't read the book.

NINA
Who do you have to blow to get a drink in this place?

Alex looks again to where Burton LaFarge was sitting, but the stool is empty.

INT. JODIE FOSTER'S APARTMENT - MIDDLE OF THE NIGHT

Alex is asleep. The phone RINGS and Alex answers it automatically. Alex checks the clock, which reads 12:12.

ALEX
(groggy)
Hello?

MEL GIBSON (O.S.)
Jodie? Did I wake you?

INT. BLACK RABBIT BAR - AN HOUR LATER

The low-lit bar is sparsely populated. Framed pencil drawings of famous and historical figures line the walls. The BARTENDER nods at Alex and then points toward the back room, where Alex finds Mel Gibson sitting over a glass of wine.

MEL GIBSON
Oh, Jodie. Thank God.

He stands and hugs Alex. They both sit down.

MEL GIBSON (CONT'D)
I'm sorry for dragging you out like this—

ALEX
(holds up her hand)
How can I help?

A WAITER approaches the table.

ALEX (CONT'D)
(to Waiter)
I'll have a glass of wine, too, please.

MEL GIBSON
I'll have another as well.

The Waiter nods and retreats.

MEL GIBSON (CONT'D)
He won't listen to me. He cannot make this movie.

ALEX
What does he say?

MEL GIBSON
Oh, you know.

He waves his hand. He's obviously a little tipsy.

MEL GIBSON (CONT'D)
He wants to do an edgier role.

ALEX
I thought I read that Leo had taken the part.

MEL GIBSON
Scheduling conflict.

Swallows the last gulp of his wine as the Waiter brings them
two new glasses. The Waiter lingers, hoping to overhear
something, but they both look up at him and he takes the hint.

ALEX
Where is he now?

MEL GIBSON
He said he was going on vacation with his family, but I think
he just doesn't want me to call again.

ALEX
I'll try him.

MEL GIBSON
He'll listen to you.

ALEX
I don't know why everyone thinks so.

MEL GIBSON
He knows Clooney trusts you.

Alex nods and sips her wine.

MEL GIBSON (CONT'D)
Anyway, there's no one else. I've done all I can.

INT. JODIE FOSTER'S APARTMENT - LATER

Alex falls back into bed. The clock reads 4:15. She stares at the ceiling and smiles. She's regained the confidence momentarily shaken by her encounter with the diner waitress.

INT. UPPER EAST SIDE APARTMENT - NIGHT

THREE COUPLES mingle, holding glasses of wine. The INDISTINCT CONVERSATION is at a LOW MURMUR. EXT. UPPER EAST SIDE BLOCK - CONTINUOUS

Alex lingers in front of a window display, killing time. She looks at her watch and sees that it's just after six. She has more time to kill. She turns back to the window display. Behind her, a GIRL passes and does a double take, recognizing her as Jodie Foster.

INT. UPPER EAST SIDE APARTMENT - CONTINUOUS

Wineglasses are refilled as the CONVERSATION GROWS A LITTLE LOUDER.

EXT. UPPER EAST SIDE APARTMENT BUILDING - CONTINUOUS

Alex glances up the face of the imposing stone building. She checks her watch again: 6:45. She breathes deeply, summoning her courage.

INT. UPPER EAST SIDE APARTMENT - CONTINUOUS

BUZZER sounds. CHRISTIANNA, the host, a sleekly dressed woman in her 50s, casually presses the button on the intercom that opens the door in the lobby, all while carrying on a conversation with her friend PILAR, another woman in her 50s.

INT. UPPER EAST SIDE APARTMENT BUILDING –
ELEVATOR - CONTINUOUS

Alex takes one last look at the list Downs gave her of those
attending the dinner, along with a quick description of each.

INT. UPPER EAST SIDE APARTMENT - CONTINUOUS

Across the room, two men are huddled around their drinks.
PAUL,60, a tall, thin, bespectacled man, is the husband of
Christianna. NATHANIEL, 60, the husband of Pilar, is stout
and well fed. They have had a few drinks and are talking in
hushed tones while glancing toward the couple on the couch:
DAVID, a roguish-looking English teacher in his 50s who
has aged well, and BRETT, a girl in her late 20s.

PAUL
What's her name again?

NATHANIEL
Brett.

Sips his drink.

PAUL
She's one of his students?

NATHANIEL
(shaking his head no)
Former.

PAUL
Jesus.

NATHANIEL
She's a big Downs fan, apparently.

PAUL
(rolls his eyes)
She's gonna love that.

A KNOCK on the door draws everyone's attention.
Christianna sets her wineglass down and opens the door on
Alex, who smiles.

CHRISTIANNA
We were beginning to wonder.

Alex steps into the apartment tentatively.

ALEX
Am I late?

CHRISTIANNA
We're just about to open a fourth bottle, if that's what you
mean.

INT. UPPER EAST SIDE APARTMENT - LIVING ROOM
- MOMENTS LATER

Alex is clustered together with David and Brett in a corner,
each holding a drink.

DAVID
Swear to God.

Alex gives an amused laugh.

BRETT
(gently but firmly)
That's not exactly right.

DAVID
Which part?

BRETT
She wasn't trying to humiliate you. You take everything so
personally.

DAVID
But she told me all this stuff was true, that it had really
happened to her, and it was word-for-word from Vivian's
first book.

BRETT
She must've known you two were friends.

DAVID
She had no way of knowing that.

BRETT
(teasing)
I seem to remember you name-dropping her in class.

David doesn't even look embarrassed by the accusation.

DAVID
The funny thing is she was a good writer in her own right.

ALEX
Yeah?

DAVID
Her work was her own, but when she told stories in
workshop, they were clearly plagiarized from published
novels. It felt like a performance piece, though no one else
seemed to catch on.

BRETT
That's what happens when they let other majors take creative
writing as an elective.

INT. UPPER EAST SIDE APARTMENT - DINING ROOM
- LATER

Everyone is sitting around the dinner table, enjoying the
sumptuous spread.

PAUL
Have they ever asked you to do anything like that before?

ALEX
(shakes her head)
No.

DAVID
They probably think this is your last book. You know, like
the last-day-of-camp ask.

NATHANIEL
(pointedly)
Or the last day of class.

David smiles at Brett, who rolls her eyes.

ALEX
Said I would.

A MURMUR of general disbelief goes around the room.

CHRISTIANNA
I've got a hundred dollars that says you don't.

PILAR
(cackling)
A thousand!

NATHANIEL
But if you're going to do a show, Charlie Austin is it.

PAUL
It'll be a ratings coup, no doubt.

CHRISTIANNA
(dismissively)
He's an interrupter.

PILAR
Oh God. It drives me crazy. And the questions aren't questions. Just things he wants to say.

DAVID
It's Socratic.

CHRISTIANNA
It's annoying.

Everyone laughs.

INT. UPPER EAST SIDE APARTMENT - LIVING ROOM - A LITTLE LATER

Everyone has been eating and drinking.

BRETT
(to Alex)
I overheard a woman on the subway raving about your new book.

Alex smiles.

BRETT (CONT'D)
I just got my copy from the Strand.

CHRISTIANNA
(to Alex)
When are we all getting our copies?

ALEX
(teasing)
It's been out for a couple of days. I assumed you'd all read it
by now.

Everyone laughs.

PAUL
Hey, we should have Jaime get us some copies.

Pushes his chair back.

CHRISTIANNA
Jaime leaves at 4. Neil is on now.

Paul picks up the receiver by the door.

PAUL
How many?

Hands around the table go up.

PAUL (CONT'D)
(into the receiver)
Hello, Neil? It's Paul in 2E. Can you do me a favor?

ALEX
(to the table)
I don't miss having a doorman.

PILAR
I still can't believe you didn't have him arrested.

ALEX
That would've just put me in the papers, where I loath to be.

BRETT
What happened?

ALEX
I had to move, is what happened.

NATHANIEL
Her doorman stole some of her letters and sold them to an autograph place.

BRETT
That's terrible.

DAVID
What did he make on that?

CHRISTIANNA
Not funny.

PILAR
He made a hundred thousand dollars before he was found out.

NATHANIEL
My doorman makes that in a year. With tips.

DAVID
Didn't the guy have some story? He needed the money for something?

ALEX
There's never a good reason for violating someone's privacy.

Paul rejoins the table.

PAUL
Neil is on it. There's a bookstore a block away.

PILAR
Did I see that Jodie Foster is going to play you in the movie?

ALEX
Yes.

NATHANIEL
What did your lawyer say about stopping it?

ALEX
Can't.

PAUL
You can sue them after the fact, if they slander you.

PILAR
Quit being a lawyer. Maybe they'll do a good job. They
wouldn't go to all the trouble of making it if they were just
going to get sued.

DAVID
No telling what their motives are.

ALEX
Except to expose me in a way I don't wish to be exposed.

BRETT
Jodie Foster is a great actor, though.

ALEX
That may be, but that still doesn't give her the right.

BRETT
Are there any movies you like?

David groans as if she's made a faux pas.

PAUL
Here we go.

PILAR
(to Brett)
Vivian has one favorite movie. And no use for any others.

BRETT
Which?

NATHANIEL
You've never heard of it.

DAVID
Hey, don't condescend.

BRETT
(wrinkles her nose in jest)
Is it really old?

They all look at Alex.

ALEX
The Lost Weekend.

Everyone is silent to gauge Brett's reaction.

BRETT
Never heard of it.

Everyone at the table erupts in laughter. Alex laughs too.

INT. UPPER EAST SIDE APARTMENT - DINING ROOM - LATER

Alex is sitting at the head of the table with a stack of copies of Downs's new book, while the others are clearing the table.

PAUL
Here's your last effort, just so you don't inscribe the new one same as the old.

Laughs and puts a copy of Downs's previous title on the table. Alex opens the book and studies the signature. While others are buzzing around cleaning and talking, she surreptitiously traces the signature and then sets to work signing the new copies. Paul is watching her carefully and looks to make sure no one else is around.

PAUL (CONT'D)
Glad to hear about the Charlie Austin thing. Makes what I have to ask you easier.

ALEX
(stops signing)
Yeah?

Paul double-checks that no one can hear them.

PAUL
(lowering his voice)
I need a favor. I promised this reporter I know, Peter Kline, that he could interview you.

ALEX
(annoyed)
I don't talk to reporters.

PAUL
You're going to talk to Charlie Austin. What's the difference?

ALEX
Charlie Austin is one thing...

PAUL
Kline really wants the interview. Just meet him for lunch,
talk to him. It'll square me with Kline.
(beat)
Don't make me remind you that you owe me one.

They trade looks.

EXT. UPPER EAST SIDE APARTMENT BUILDING -
LATER THAT NIGHT

Alex exits and walks briskly down the street. She turns the
corner and slows down. She pulled it off.

INT. MAXWELL JAY'S - STILL LATER

Alex is at her now usual place at the bar. The bar is mostly
empty, as it's late. The muted TV is on above. The Bartender
pours Alex another drink.

BARTENDER
Celebrating?

ALEX
You could say that.

BARTENDER
I'll join you. Just found out my girlfriend is not pregnant.

Alex laughs as the Bartender pours himself half a beer. Over
the Bartender's shoulder, on the TV, looms the face of Burton
LaFarge, the screenwriter Alex previously met at the bar.
Some kind of news item.

ALEX
(pointing at the TV)
Isn't that the guy who comes in here?

Bartender looks at the TV.

BARTENDER
Didn't realize that the first time I saw it. Looks like him,
yeah. Wild.

ALEX
What happened?

BARTENDER
Pushed under a train.

Alex continues to watch the muted news story.

BARTENDER (CONT'D)
Grand Central. Probably some crazy. I always stand with my
back to the train.

Alex nods, half listening, still staring at the television. Jessica
enters the bar and makes her way to Alex, smiling
triumphantly at the Bartender.

BARTENDER (CONT'D)
Hello, Jessica.

JESSICA
(pointedly)
Long time no see, Jeremy.

She gives Alex a peck on the cheek.

ALEX
You made it.

JESSICA
Was working late anyway. Glad you called.

INT. MAXWELL JAY'S - AN HOUR LATER

Alex and Jessica are two of the last in the bar.

ALEX
What's after this?

JESSICA
Home, I guess.

ALEX
Come back with me.

JESSICA
Is that a command or a question?

ALEX
Come back with me?

She smiles. Jessica looks at her, considering, scrutinizing her, making up her mind.

JESSICA
Maybe.

ALEX
Maybe. Not as promising as a yes, but not as devastating as a no.

She smiles.

INT. JODIE FOSTER'S APARTMENT - BEDROOM - THAT NIGHT

Jessica is in bed. Alex enters from the bathroom, and undresses. Jessica watches intently, comparing. Alex slips into bed and they kiss, soft at first and then hard. Jessica takes Alex's arm and wraps it around her.

JESSICA
Hold me like this again.

Alex complies, follows her lead. They kiss some more. Alex kisses Jessica's neck and she moans. Jessica suddenly rolls Alex onto her back and flips on top of her.

JESSICA (CONT'D)
(deviously)
Like last time.

ALEX
(repeating)
Like last time.

She smiles and pulls Jessica to her.

INT. JODIE FOSTER'S APARTMENT - BEDROOM - LATER

Alex and Jessica are in bed, asleep. There's a KNOCK at the door. Alex startles awake.

JESSICA
What is it?

ALEX
Someone's at the door.

JESSICA
Are you sure?

Alex gets out of bed and puts on a T-shirt.

ALEX
It's probably just the doorman.

INT. JODIE FOSTER'S APARTMENT - LIVING ROOM -
CONTINUOUS

Another KNOCK just as Alex swings the door open to find
DETECTIVE DEGNER, a man in his 50s, and DETECTIVE
KEPHART, a woman in her 40s. Detective Degner flashes a
badge.

DETECTIVE DEGNER
I'm sorry to bother you, Ms. Foster, especially this time of
night.

ALEX
What's this about?

DETECTIVE KEPHART
Can we come in?

INT. JODIE FOSTER'S APARTMENT - LIVING ROOM
- MOMENTS LATER

Alex is sitting in a chair while the two detectives are on the
couch. Alex is holding the photo of Burton LaFarge she saw
earlier on the television.

DETECTIVE DEGNER
You've never seen him?

ALEX
(thinking)
I was telling the bartender at Maxwell Jay's that it looked
like someone who drank there.

DETECTIVE KEPHART
Nice place. You a regular?

ALEX
Semi.

DETECTIVE DEGNER
And you saw this Burton LaFarge there?

ALEX
Yes.

DETECTIVE KEPHART
Did you drink with him at Maxwell Jay's?

ALEX
I saw him there once or twice.

DETECTIVE KEPHART
Recently?

ALEX
I'm not exactly sure. The bartender probably has a better sense of that. I sometimes can't tell what day of the week it is.

Gives a weak smile.

DETECTIVE KEPHART
We'll ask him.

Awkward pause.

ALEX
You mean you haven't already spoken with him?

DETECTIVE KEPHART
We didn't know anything about the connection with the bar until you told us.

ALEX
(confused)
Then how did you get here?

The detectives give each other a look. Detective Degner takes a piece of paper out of his jacket pocket and hands it to Alex. The slip of paper reads: "Ask Jodie Foster"

Alex stares at the paper. Has no idea how to react.

DETECTIVE DEGNER
That was on the body.

DETECTIVE KEPHART
So you can see why we're confused.

DETECTIVE DEGNER
Can you say where you were at about ten o'clock?

Alex thinks, realizing that Jodie Foster doesn't have an alibi, since everyone at the dinner party knew her as Vivian Downs.

ALEX
At the movies.

DETECTIVE DEGNER
Movie stub?

Alex shakes her head.

DETECTIVE DEGNER (CONT'D)
What did you see?

ALEX
Vertigo. At the Hitchcock revival downtown.

DETECTIVE KEPHART
Love Hitchcock.

Jessica appears from the bedroom.

ALEX
This is Jessica.

JESSICA
What's wrong?

ALEX
Someone was pushed under a train.

JESSICA
Oh my God.

ALEX
Said he knows me.

Hands the note to her. She takes it and reads it.

JESSICA
Who was it?

DETECTIVE DEGNER
A screenwriter. Burton LaFarge.

JESSICA
(to Alex)
Someone you worked with?

Alex shakes her head no.

JESSICA (CONT'D)
(to the detectives)
Any idea who did it?

The detectives have been watching this back-and-forth carefully. Always suspicious.

DETECTIVE KEPHART
The CCTV in the station caught an image of the assailant, but he or she was dressed in black and wearing a black hood.

DETECTIVE DEGNER
At the moment the victim is pushed, the assailant's wrist can be seen. Whoever it was, they have a tattoo of a star on their wrist.

Beat.

Alex and Jessica absorb this information. Alex involuntarily looks at her wrists, as do the detectives.

DETECTIVE KEPHART
(to Jessica)
Mind showing me your wrists?

Jessica is taken aback but raises her arms so that her robe slides away revealing her wrists. Nothing.

DETECTIVE KEPHART (CONT'D)
Thank you.

The detectives rise, and Alex does too.

DETECTIVE DEGNER
Sorry again to have bothered you at this hour.

ALEX
I'm sorry we couldn't help.

DETECTIVE KEPHART
We may call on you again.

ALEX
Of course.

DETECTIVE KEPHART
Also, if you don't mind my saying this, I just saw Panic
Room and it was terrific.

ALEX
Thank you. That's a nice thing to hear.

DETECTIVE KEPHART
Good night.

The detectives nod at Jessica. Alex lets them out.

JESSICA
What a weird thing.

Alex looks at her, as if debating. But she's a little freaked out
and wants an ally, so she opens a drawer and takes out the
script given her by Burton LaFarge and tosses it on the coffee
table. Jessica sees the title page and backs away from it as if
it were explosive.

JESSICA (CONT'D)
Why didn't you say anything?

ALEX
(panicked)
I don't know. Instinct.
(beat)

I met the guy once.
(corrects herself)
Twice.

They both stare at the screenplay on the coffee table.

JESSICA
We'll deal with it in the morning.

INT. JODIE FOSTER'S APARTMENT - BEDROOM -
LATER

Alex lies in bed staring at the ceiling, unable to sleep. Jessica
is on her side, staring at the wall, also unable to sleep.

JESSICA
Are you going to meet that reporter for lunch?

ALEX
Seems like a bad idea.

JESSICA
Maybe he knows something more about all of this.

Alex continues to stare at the ceiling, unable to sleep. She
closes her eyes and we hear the SOUND OF A SUBWAY IN
MOTION as the scene dissolves.

EXT. SUBWAY TRAIN - DAY

Alex stands in the noisy car. Glimpses headline on the
newspaper of a seated commuter: "Man Pushed Under
Train."

INT. JACKSON'S BISTRO - A LITTLE LATER

Alex walks into the darkened restaurant, letting her eyes

adjust. PETER KLINE, in his late 40s, waves from a table against the wall. He stands when Alex approaches.

PETER
Peter Kline.

ALEX
Vivian Downs.

They sit.

PETER
Thanks for meeting me.

ALEX
I owe Paul a favor.

PETER
(amused)
I wondered.

INT. JACKSON'S BISTRO - LATER

Lunch is being cleared by the WAITER.

ALEX
What might not be true is that people assume I wrote my last book for reasons other than the simple fact that it was a book that I needed to write. But other than that, people just write what they want to write.

Peter considers this answer, which ends the interview.

PETER
Coffee?

ALEX
Sure.

Peter nods at the Waiter, who goes for the coffee.

Beat.

PETER
I have to say, it's an impressive performance.

ALEX
Which?

The Waiter sets the coffee in front of them. Peter takes a sip, staring at Alex over the cup.

PETER
Don't worry. I won't say anything.

Alex looks fearful.

ALEX
To whom about what?

Peter waves to someone behind Alex, who turns and sees two people she recognizes as Detective Degner and Detective Kephart.

PETER
Colleagues. This is an old newspaper hangout.

Detective Degner and Detective Kephart take a table on the other side of the room from them.

ALEX
I don't—

PETER
Yeah, sorry about that. Years of trying to get the scoop clouds my thinking sometimes. I was hoping you'd tell them something useful. Or printable. Saw the thing about the tattoo on the news and thought it might sell it.

Reaches into his bag and produces the same note the detectives showed her that night: "Ask Jodie Foster."

ALEX
Where did you get that?

PETER
I wrote it.

Alex gives him a look.

PETER (CONT'D)
Or transcribed it, I should say. Burton left that message on my answering machine the day before he died.

ALEX
Why?

PETER
He came to me about a month ago with an interesting story about how Vivian Downs had plagiarized him for her new book. The one that just came out.

ALEX
That's ludicrous.

PETER
It's a bit outlandish. But Burton said he had proof. He was going to show it to me, but then there was an unfortunate accident.

ALEX
What was the proof?

PETER
He didn't say. But he seemed to suggest that Jodie Foster
knows.

ALEX
Well, it's libel. Good thing you didn't run with it. My
lawyers have an impressive winning streak.

Beat.

PETER
You mean Vivian Downs's lawyers do.

Awkward silence as Alex realizes that Peter knows she's not
Vivian Downs.

PETER (CONT'D)
The resemblance is pretty remarkable, I have to admit. And I
didn't put it together until I was having lunch with my old
college roommate a week or so ago. He's a casting agent.
And he told me about this actor he'd seen who was the
spitting image of Jodie Foster.
(beat)
Who for some reason is impersonating Vivian Downs.

Alex eyes him coolly.

ALEX
Talk about outlandish stories.

PETER
My friend told me the actor's name, but I've forgotten it. I
could ask him again, I guess. My readers might be interested
in that story.

Beat.

ALEX
What do you want?

PETER
I want the truth about Vivian Downs and her new book.

ALEX
Why do you care?

PETER
Let's just say I have a personal interest in the matter.

Alex considers this and debates telling him something.

ALEX
(reluctantly)
There's a letter.

PETER
What kind of letter?

ALEX
LaFarge mailed a letter to my—to Downs's editor, detailing his accusations.

PETER
Have you read it?

Alex shakes her head no.

PETER (CONT'D)
If you can get me that letter, we'll forget all this other business, as interesting as it might be to my readers.

ALEX
How am I supposed to do that?

Peter stands.

PETER
You seem like a resourceful person.

The fake detectives at the other table glance up.

ALEX
I can't—

PETER
I've got two interesting stories to choose from. And I don't
care which one I tell, but my deadline either way is the end of
the week.
(beat)
Lunch was on the paper, by the way.

Peter pats Alex on the back and waves to the fake detectives
as he exits. Alex stares in disbelief at Peter's empty seat.

INT. JODIE FOSTER'S APARTMENT - LATER

Alex enters and finds Jessica lying on the couch, reading the
screenplay Burton LaFarge gave her.

JESSICA
You obviously didn't read this.

ALEX
Why would I?

JESSICA
Oh, I don't know. It's just the story of an unknown writer
whose work is stolen by a famous author.

ALEX
What?

JESSICA
But the writer is killed in what looks like an accident—

ALEX
(incredulous)
Pushed under a train?

JESSICA
Falls down an elevator shaft. At the famous author's publishing house.

Alex processes this information.

ALEX
Why does he go to the publishing house?

JESSICA
I think you know.

ALEX
To give the editor a letter?

JESSICA
(covers her mouth)
Oh my God.

ALEX
Then what?

Jessica flips through the pages as she recounts the plot.

JESSICA
He tips off a journalist, who is really the bitter, jilted ex-college boyfriend of the famous author's daughter.

ALEX
(thinking)
Really.

JESSICA
They were engaged, but she broke it off. Anyway, the writer
is paranoid and thinks he's being followed. The famous
author's book is about to be published, and the writer knows
he's a liability.

Alex sits down on the couch next to her and puts her head in
her hands.

ALEX
Jesus.

JESSICA
You haven't even heard the best part. He makes friends with
the actor playing the famous author in an upcoming movie
before he's killed.

Alex moans.

JESSICA (CONT'D)
And the actor is sympathetic to the writer and avenges his
death by helping catch the famous author.

ALEX
How does she do that?

JESSICA
She gets the letter from the editor and gives it to the
journalist.

Alex is astounded by this.

ALEX
How?

JESSICA
She goes to the publishing house at night. pretending to be
the famous author and tells the security guard she left
something in her editor's office.

Alex takes this in, thinking.

ALEX
Does he name the security guard?

INT. VIVIAN DOWNS'S APARTMENT - DAY

Downs and Alex are sitting across from each other, as in their
first meeting. Alex is turning over a snow globe from Florida
while Downs looks on. Veronica is in the background,
making coffee in the kitchen.

ALEX
Relaxing trip?

DOWNS
Yes, very.

ALEX
Get any sun?

Veronica sets down a coffee cup for each of them. Alex
notices that her wrist is wrapped in a bandage.

DOWNS
I'm not really the beach type.

ALEX
(to Veronica)
What happened?

VERONICA
It's nothing.

DOWNS
So? How did it go? Were you convincing?

ALEX
Everyone except Deanna, the diner waitress, I think.

DOWNS
She's naturally suspicious. Comes with the trade. What about
Christianna's dinner party?

Alex waits a beat. Downs seems keen on the answer.

ALEX
No problems.

DOWNS
(delighted)
It's amazing how little attention people pay, is it not? I mean
outside of the attention they pay to themselves.

ALEX
There was one thing.

DOWNS
Oh?

ALEX
One of the dinner guests. Paul?

DOWNS
Saint Paul, yes.

ALEX
He said you owed him a favor and wanted it paid in the form
of lunch with a reporter, Peter Kline.

A long pause is broken by a CLATTERING in the
background. Veronica has dropped something in the kitchen.

DOWNS
And how is Peter?

ALEX
He has an interest in you.

DOWNS
It's not me he's interested in.

Looks off toward the kitchen.

ALEX
So I gathered.

DOWNS
Was he convinced?

Alex pauses, letting the question float between them. How
she answers will determine the course of action she'll take.

ALEX
Seemed to be.

This pleases Downs.

ALEX (CONT'D)
Oh, and your editor cornered me about appearing on Charlie
Austin.

DOWNS
(amused)
Nothing I can't undo.

Beat. The interview is over, and Downs puts her hands on the
armrests of her chair, as if to rise, but doesn't when Alex
shows no sign of doing the same.

ALEX
You may have missed the news while you were away. A man
was pushed under a train.

DOWNS
(resignedly)
This city.

ALEX
I actually met him a few days prior.

DOWNS
Oh?

ALEX
He was a writer, too.

Downs gives a dismissive look.

DOWNS
The world is full of writers, seems.

ALEX
He showed me some of his work.

Downs gives a surprised look.

ALEX (CONT'D)
A screenplay.

DOWNS
(relieved)
I'm guessing you get a lot of that.

ALEX
Yes.

DOWNS
As do I.

ALEX
Anything interesting?

DOWNS
I make it a practice not to read anything sent to me. The work of others must remain behind a wall, for their protection and for mine. I imagine the same is true for you.

ALEX
I made an exception in this case.

DOWNS
Exceptions can become precedent. Very dangerous.

ALEX
True.

DOWNS
I worry an exception would do great damage to my reputation. When you've spent your life curating your reputation, you're loath to have some nobody from nowhere wreck it with carelessness.

ALEX
It must be wearying, that kind of vigilance.

DOWNS
A golden cage, don't you find?

EXT. VIVIAN DOWNS'S APARTMENT BUILDING - A
LITTLE LATER

Veronica exits the building. Alex is across the street and
crosses over to her as she starts to walk down the sidewalk.
Veronica looks terrified when she sees Alex. She doesn't
stop, and Alex walks alongside her.

VERONICA
You scared me.

ALEX
I didn't mean to.

VERONICA
What do you want?

ALEX
I just want to talk to you.

VERONICA
I don't have anything to say.

ALEX
Peter is out to get your mother.

Veronica stops and turns to face her, a quizzical look on her
face.

VERONICA
Poor Peter.

ALEX
Why does he hate your mother?

VERONICA
It's me he hates. He wants to hurt me.

ALEX
There's something going on and it may involve your mother.

Veronica gives her a strange look.

ALEX (CONT'D)
There's a letter that connects your mother to the writer that
was pushed under the train.

VERONICA
(fearfully)
I'm sure she doesn't know anything about that.

ALEX
She's involved, Veronica.

VERONICA
She could never be involved in something like that.

ALEX
I know she's your mother and it's hard to hear, but I think
she's a bad person.

VERONICA
A bad person? You don't know anything about her. Would a
bad person help Mike the way my mother helped him when
he was in trouble?

ALEX
What kind of trouble?

VERONICA
Please stay away from me and my mother.

Turns to go, but Alex grabs her by her bandaged wrist.

ALEX
I had a friend who had a tattoo removed. Said it hurt like hell.

Alex unravels the bandage as Veronica tries to squirm free.
Alex is expecting to see the fresh scar of a removed tattoo,
but it's just a burn. Veronica storms off.

INT. JODIE FOSTER'S APARTMENT - DAY

Alex enters to find Jessica with her bag packed, making one
last check of the place.

ALEX
What happened?

JESSICA
More cops. Different ones, who had never heard of the first
ones.

She nods toward a business card on the side table.
Alex reads the card: J.D. Martens, Homicide Detective.

JESSICA (CONT'D)
Asked me a bunch of questions I didn't know the answers to.

She's clearly rattled.

JESSICA (CONT'D)
Said they'd be back.

ALEX
Did they say when?

Jessica zips up her bag.

JESSICA
You should go too.

ALEX
Go where?

JESSICA
Wherever.

ALEX
Is that where you're going?

Jessica stops what she's doing and looks at her.

JESSICA
It's better if we don't know where each other is.

Alex is a little frightened by her behavior.

ALEX
Slow down. Tell me what's happened.

JESSICA
It's not what's happened. It's what is happening.

ALEX
Tell me.

JESSICA
(a little frantic)
It's partly my fault. But I had no idea—

ALEX
No idea about what?

Jessica gives her a long look.

JESSICA
That day when you found me, I was picking up my things.
Jodie wanted me to clear out my stuff while she was gone. I
begged her for a second chance, but I could see it was over.

Alex realizes what she's saying.

JESSICA (CONT'D)
Yeah, okay, I knew. But I'd promised that Jodie would show
up for the fund-raiser at work, and I needed you to save face.
(beat)
And the rest of it was... I'm a curious person, let's just say.
Which is at the root of all my problems. Jodie understood
that, until one day she didn't. But whatever is happening now
is bad and we should both move on.

ALEX
It's going to be fine. I'll go to the police and tell them
everything. I'll give them the script and they'll see that we
had nothing to do with any of this.

JESSICA
I burned the script.

ALEX
(rising panic in her voice)
Why? Why would you do that?

JESSICA
It connects us to this mess. Now we're free to go. Don't you
see?

Alex sinks onto the couch.

JESSICA (CONT'D)
What?

Alex looks at her. Wants to confide in her that she's not free of the situation, but doesn't.

ALEX
Nothing. You should go.

Jessica gives her a last look and exits.

INT. MAXWELL JAY'S - NIGHT

Alex is sitting at the bar with a drink. The place is packed. CUSTOMERS keep glancing over at Alex, recognizing her as Jodie Foster. The late news plays on the television, and Alex reads the closed captioning: "Full CCTV Video of Victim Being Pushed Under Train Released to the Public." Alex watches the video, which has been slowed down. In the top corner, at the far end of the platform, she sees Vivian Downs wearing the same shirt Alex wore when she first met Downs at her apartment. Downs is also not wearing her glasses, trying to look as much like Jodie Foster as possible. In the video Downs stares straight ahead as LaFarge is pushed, not reacting like the others do as LaFarge screams out. Startled, Alex leaves the bar, pushing her way through the crowd of customers, who recognize her as she passes.

EXT. PUBLISHING HOUSE - NIGHT

Alex approaches the building.

INT. PUBLISHING HOUSE LOBBY - CONTINUOUS

Alex approaches the security desk. The security guard, a large man, looks up. Alex notes his name tag: C. BOCK. They exchange a look.

BOCK
You here for the thing you forgot in your editor's office?

ALEX
Uh-huh.

Bock checks to see that no one else is around and opens the
drawer of his desk. He takes out his metal lunch box and
opens it. Under a false bottom he procures an envelope and
hands it to Alex.

BOCK
The original was shredded. This is just a copy.

ALEX
Okay.

BOCK
I'm glad to have that in someone else's hands. Especially
after what happened to Burton.

ALEX
Did you know him well?

BOCK
We went to graduate school together.

ALEX
You're a writer too?

BOCK
Nah. I turned out just to be a reader. Which makes this a
pretty good job.

ALEX
The world needs readers, too.

BOCK
No one wanted it more than Burton. When I got the job here, he would buy me lunch in the cafeteria upstairs, just to be near the action.

Looks sadly at the envelope.

BOCK (CONT'D)
That's his last chance to be published.

Alex nods grimly.

ALEX
Can I count on you if I need to?

BOCK
(shakes his head no)
I can't get involved, sorry. I've got my own problems.

INT. VIVIAN DOWNS'S APARTMENT - DAY

Downs opens the door and is surprised to find Alex.

DOWNS
What is it?

ALEX
We need to talk.

DOWNS
Not today. I'm busy.

ALEX
This can't wait.

Pushes her way into the apartment.

DOWNS
My worst nightmare come true.

ALEX
Not yet.

Sits at the kitchen table. Downs sits reluctantly.

DOWNS
What do you want?

ALEX
I know about Burton LaFarge.

DOWNS
What of him?

ALEX
It's going to come out. Peter Kline is going to make sure of
it.

Downs regards him.

DOWNS
I've handled Mr. Kline in the past, and could again. Besides,
it's just LaFarge's word against mine. And he's no longer
with us.

ALEX
Conveniently.

Downs gets up and goes to a nearby closet. She opens it and
removes a small cardboard box. She places the box on the
table and sits back down. Alex sees that the box is from
Burton LaFarge, addressed to Downs.

ALEX (CONT'D)
What is it?

DOWNS
I'm afraid the price of knowing the answer is too high.

Alex reacts.

ALEX
When did he send it?

DOWNS
(nonchalantly)
Oh, about the same time he started sending letters accusing
me of this and that.

ALEX
Why didn't you take it to the police?

DOWNS
It wouldn't Have made sense to be so proactive. Narratively,
I mean.

ALEX
(thinking out loud)
Better to hold on to it and present it as a defense against
LaFarge's claims.

DOWNS
They say novels can't compete with real life. I have to say,
sometimes I agree.

Pushes the box aside.

DOWNS (CONT'D)
For instance, the fiction you've been perpetrating.

Alex starts.

ALEX
I have no idea what—

Downs picks up the box and replaces it in the closet.

DOWNS
The problem with coincidence is that most times it isn't
believable. Character A in a story needs X to happen, but true
to life X doesn't happen. But then some random act occurs
and suddenly X is realized.

ALEX
What random act?

DOWNS
My having lunch in a Midtown restaurant I don't normally
frequent.

Alex considers this.

DOWNS (CONT'D)
And who else do I see at this restaurant? An Academy
award-winning actor lunching with a companion.

INSERT: Scene where Alex and Karen are having lunch.
Jared is taking their order. Pull back to reveal Downs sitting
at another table in the far corner.

DOWNS (CONT'D)
I'm not easily starstruck, but what a coincidence.

ALEX
What coincidence?

DOWNS
I'd been expending an extraordinary amount of energy
thinking about Jodie Foster, and here she appears at lunch.
(beat)
Remarkable.
(beat)
But even more remarkable is that in short order Jodie Foster
reveals herself to be but a mirage.

INSERT: Back-and-forth when Karen tells Jared that Alex
isn't Jodie Foster.

DOWNS (CONT'D)
What a strange curse, to so closely resemble someone so well
known in your own chosen field.

Alex is stunned into muteness.

DOWNS (CONT'D)
My own resemblance to Jodie Foster is a bit of a debate. I
don't see it, but others do. But for you it must be a constant
irritation. Or worse.
(beat)
I suppose it was simple curiosity that made me follow you
from the restaurant.

ALEX
Rather a dull way to spend the day.

DOWNS
Perhaps. But it was addicting to see how your curse affected
your day-to-day life.

INSERT: Scene where Alex signs author for the tourists.
Reveal that Downs is watching from nearby.

DOWNS (CONT'D)
But then, of course, your path was altered.

INSERT: Scene in front of Jodie Foster's building where the Doorman mistakes Alex for Foster.

DOWNS (CONT'D)
My disappointment was only momentary. I suddenly realized the wonderful opportunity I'd been given.

INSERT: Phone conversation between Downs and Alex. Reveal that Downs is calling from a pay phone on the street below.

ALEX
You want me to believe that you dreamed up all of this stuff on the spot?

Downs shrugs.

DOWNS
When your life revolves around narrative, plots are not hard to come by.
(beat)
Here's another plausible plot: A not-very-good actor who looks like another, more talented and more famous actor uses that resemblance as an excuse for her inability to realize her aspirations.

Alex is stunned.

DOWNS (CONT'D)
And let's not forget our latest plot: poor Jodie Foster. Dreamed of being an actor, put in the work, only to have a talentless nobody steal her reputation and all that she's achieved.

Alex looks like she wants to disagree but can't.

DOWNS (CONT'D)
And for what? So you could know what it's like to be
famous? So you could feel like a real actor, even if you're
not?

ALEX
Everyone believed—

Downs waves her off.

DOWNS
That's less about your acting skills and more about people's
inattention.

There's a KNOCK at the door, and Downs's son-in-law
MIKE enters. He gives a cowed look, as if he's embarrassed
at interrupting.

DOWNS (CONT'D)
Mike. You know...
(looks at Alex)
What is your name?

ALEX
Alex.

DOWNS
Huh.

Mike gives a halfhearted wave, and Alex notices the star
tattoo on the inside of his wrist.

MIKE
Veronica said you wanted to see me.

DOWNS
Yes, Alex was just leaving.

Alex gets up and goes to the door, keeping her eye on Mike.
Downs trails her.

DOWNS (CONT'D)
I expect our paths won't meet again.

Alex gives her a questioning look as Downs closes the door.

INT. JODIE FOSTER'S APARTMENT – THAT
AFTERNOON

The Doorman opens the door and sets down a couple of
suitcases, then goes out again, closing the door.

INT. SUBWAY STATION - THAT AFTERNOON

Peter Kline is standing on the platform with a crowd of other
straphangers, waiting for the train. Lost in the crowd, many
people deep, is Mike, who is staring at Kline. The train
ROARS into the station.

INT. JODIE FOSTER'S APARTMENT BUILDING -
LOBBY – THAT AFTERNOON

Alex enters and the Doorman waves.

DOORMAN
All taken care of, sir.

Alex nods as if she knows what the Doorman means, though
she doesn't.

INT. JODIE FOSTER'S APARTMENT - MOMENTS
LATER

Alex enters and is startled to see the suitcases. In a panic, she
begins packing up her meager belongings. The door opens
and Jodie Foster walks in with Mel Gibson.

ALEX
I can explain.

SUPER: A MONTH LATER

INT. VIVIAN DOWNS'S APARTMENT – LATE
AFTERNOON

Downs is seated, watching an entertainment news program
on television.

TV ANCHOR (O.S.)
Production of the film based on the life of celebrated novelist
Vivian Downs, starring Academy award-winning actor Jodie
Foster, has been moved up to capitalize on the recent news
involving charges of plagiarism by another writer, who was
subsequently pushed under a Midtown subway train. Peter
Kline, the reporter who broke the story, has been hired as a
consultant.

INSERT: Scene where Kline and Mike are on the platform.

Mike approaches Kline and gives him an envelope, the letter.

INSERT: Scene where Alex approaches Mike coming out of
Downs's apartment building. They sit in the window of the
coffee shop. Alex is doing all the talking. Mike is
listening, his head down, nodding. Alex passes him the letter.
Downs gets up and goes to the closet where she keeps the
box from LaFarge.

TV ANCHOR (O.S.) (CONT'D)
Producers have also announced plans to include the bizarre true-life story of Alex North, the out-of-work actor bearing a resemblance to Jodie Foster who impersonated both Foster and Downs for a number of weeks before the deception was uncovered.

INSERT: Footage from entertainment news channel:

JARED
She pretended to be Jodie Foster and gave me her autograph.

JEREMY
Had no idea. Chick must be a good actor.

DEANNA
You could tell something was off. It makes sense now.

KAREN
She's not a bad person, not the person you're making her out to be. If you're watching, Alex, please let me or someone know if you're okay.

Downs sits down again and puts the box on the coffee table in front of him. She picks up a remote and switches off the TV. She sits with the box in front of her for a long moment. She stares at the box, then out the window. She's ready.

EXT. VIVIAN DOWNS'S APARTMENT BUILDING - CONTINUOUS

TWO DETECTIVES flash their badges at the building's SUPERINTENDENT. The Super points up the stairs.

INT. VIVIAN DOWNS'S APARTMENT - CONTINUOUS

Downs takes out a pocketknife and slices off the return

address from Burton LaFarge and burns it in an ashtray. She watches the embers die out. She cuts open the box, carefully folds the knife and sets it on the table. There's a KNOCK at the door, but it doesn't startle her. She's been expecting it. She reaches for the box to open it.

EXT. DESERT - DAY

An old pickup truck pulls into an unpaved parking lot in front of a diner, kicking up a tornado of dust.

INT. DINER – CONTINUOUS

The DRIVER takes a seat at the counter. The WAITRESS smiles at him as a BELL DINGS.

WAITRESS
Be there in a minute, darling.

She saunters to the corner booth, where Alex is seated, alone, looking at the paper. The headline says: "Celebrated Novelist Victim of Anthrax." The article has a picture of Vivian Downs. Alex turns the paper over when the Waitress sets down the food.

WAITRESS (CONT'D)
Can I get you anything else?

ALEX
I'm good, thanks.

Waitress writes out her check and sets it on the table. Goes to take the Driver's order.

Alex leaves cash for the bill and leaves.

DRIVER
Who was that?

WAITRESS
She's the one interested in buying Old Man Fuller's place.

DRIVER
She looks like that actor, the one in the news.

WAITRESS
Told her the same thing. Says she doesn't watch the movies.

They both look out the window as Alex gets into her car and drives away.

DRIVER
What's good today?

THE END

Jaime Clarke is a graduate of the University of Arizona and holds an MFA from Bennington College. He is the author of the novels *We're So Famous, Vernon Downs,* and *World Gone Water*; editor of the anthologies *Don't You Forget About Me: Contemporary Writers on the Films of John Hughes, Conversations with Jonathan Lethem,* and *Talk Show: On the Couch with Contemporary Writers*; and co-editor of the anthologies *No Near Exit: Writers Select Their Favorite Work from Post Road Magazine* (with Mary Cotton), and *Boston Noir 2: The Classics* (with Dennis Lehane and Mary Cotton). He is a founding editor of the literary magazine *Post Road*, now published at Boston College, and co-owner, with his wife, of Newtonville Books, an independent bookstore in Boston.

By the same author

Vernon Downs: A Novel
by Jaime Clarke

"*Vernon Downs* is a gripping, hypnotically written and unnerving look at the dark side of literary adulation. Jaime Clarke's tautly suspenseful novel is a cautionary tale for writers and readers alike–after finishing it, you may start to think that J.D. Salinger had the right idea after all."
–Tom Perrotta, author of *Election*, *Little Children*, and *The Leftovers*

"Moving and edgy in just the right way. Love (or lack of) and Family (or lack of) is at the heart of this wonderfully obsessive novel." – Gary Shteyngart, author of *Super Sad True Love Story*

"All strong literature stems from obsession. *Vernon Downs* belongs to a tradition that includes Nicholson Baker's *U and I*, Geoff Dyer's *Out of Sheer Rage*, and—for that matter—*Pale Fire*. What makes Clarke's excellent novel stand out isn't just its rueful intelligence, or its playful semi-veiling of certain notorious literary figures, but its startling sadness. *Vernon Downs* is first rate." —Matthew Specktor, author of *American Dream Machine*

"*Vernon Downs* is a brilliant meditation on obsession, art, and celebrity. Charlie Martens's mounting fixation with the titular Vernon is not only driven by the burn of heartbreak and the lure of fame, but also a lost young man's struggle to locate his place in the world. *Vernon Downs* is an intoxicating novel, and Clarke is a dazzling literary talent."
— Laura van den Berg, author of *The Isle of Youth*

"An engrossing novel about longing and impersonation, which is to say, a story about the distance between persons, distances within ourselves. Clarke's prose is infused with music and intelligence and deep feeling." — Charles Yu, author of *Sorry Please Thank You*

"*Vernon Downs* is a fascinating and sly tribute to a certain fascinating and sly writer, but this novel also perfectly captures the lonely distortions of a true obsession." — Dana Spiotta, author of *Stone Arabia*

Selected by *The Millions* as a Most Anticipated Read

"Though *Vernon Downs* appears to be about deception and celebrity, it's really about the alienation out of which these things grow. Clarke shows that obsession is, at root, about yearning: about the things we don't have but desperately want; about our longing to be anyone but ourselves.
– *The Boston Globe*

"A stunning and unsettling foray into a glamorous world of celebrity writers, artistic loneliness, and individual desperation." – *The Harvard Crimson*

"*Vernon Downs* is a fast-moving and yet, at times, quite sad book about, in the broadest sense, longing."
– *The Brooklyn Rail*

World Gone Water: A Novel
by Jaime Clarke

"Jaime Clarke's *World Gone Water* is so fresh and daring, a necessary book, a barbaric yawp that revels in its taboo: the sexual and emotional desires of today's hetero young man. Clarke is a sure and sensitive writer, his line are clean and carry us right to the tender heart of his lovelorn hero, Charlie Martens. This is the book Hemingway and Kerouac would want to read. It's the sort of honesty in this climate that many of us aren't brave enough to write." – Tony D'Souza, author of *The Konkans*.

"This unsettling novel ponders human morality and sexuality, and the murky interplay between the two. Charlie Martens is a compelling anti-hero with a voice that can turn on a dime, from shrugging naiveté to chilling frankness. *World Gone Water* is a candid, often startling portrait of an unconventional life."— J. Robert Lennon, author of *Familiar*

"Funny and surprising, *World Gone Water* is terrific fun to read ... and, as a spectacle of bad behavior, pretty terrifying to contemplate." –- Adrienne Miller, author of *The Coast of Akron*

"Charlie Martens is my favorite kind of narrator, an obsessive yearner whose commitment to his worldview is so overwhelming that the distance between his words and the reader's usual thinking gets clouded fast. *World Gone Water* will draw you in, make you complicit, and finally leave you both discomfited and thrilled." — Matt Bell, author of *In the House upon the Dirt between the Lake and the Woods*

"Charlie Martens will make you laugh. More, he'll offend and shock you while making you laugh. Even trickier: he'll somehow make you like him, root for him, despite yourself and despite him. This novel travels into the dark heart of male/female relations and yet there is tenderness, humanity, hope. Jaime Clarke rides what is a terribly fine line between hero and antihero. Read and be astounded."
– Amy Grace Loyd, author of *The Affairs of Others*

Garden Lakes: A Novel
by Jaime Clarke

"It takes some nerve to revisit a bulletproof classic, but Jaime Clarke does so, with elegance and a cool contemporary eye, in this cunningly crafted homage to *Lord of the Flies*. He understands all too well the complex psychology of boyhood, how easily the insecurities and power plays slide into mayhem when adults look the other way."

— Julia Glass, National Book Award-winning author of *Three Junes*

"Jaime Clarke reminds us that if the banality of evil is indeed a viable truth, its seeds are most likely sewn among adolescent boys."

— Brad Watson, author of *Aliens in the Prime of Their Lives*

"In the flawlessly imagined *Garden Lakes*, Jaime Clarke pays homage to *Lord of the Flies* and creates his own vivid, inadvertently isolated community. As summer tightens its grip, and adult authority recedes, his boys gradually reveal themselves to scary and exhilarating effect. In the hands of this master of suspense and psychological detail, the result is a compulsively readable novel."

— Margot Livesey, author of *The Flight of Gemma Hardy*

"Smart, seductive, and suggestively sinister, *Garden Lakes* is a disturbingly honest look at how our lies shape our lives and destroy our communities. Read it: Part three in one of the best literary trilogies we have."

— Scott Cheshire, author of *High as the Horses' Bridles*

"As tense and tight and pitch-perfect as Clarke's narrative of the harrowing events at *Garden Lakes* is, and as fine a meditation it is on Golding's novel, what deepens this book to another level of insight and artfulness is the parallel portrait of Charlie Martens as an adult, years after his fateful role that summer, still tyrannized, paralyzed, tangled in lies, wishing for redemption, maybe fated never to get it. Complicated and feral, *Garden Lakes* is thrilling, literary, and smart as hell."

– Paul Harding, Pulitzer Prize-winning author of *Tinkers*

We're So Famous: A Novel
by Jaime Clarke

"Jaime Clarke pulls off a sympathetic act of sustained male imagination: entering the minds of innocent teenage girls dreaming of fame. A glibly surreal world where the only thing wanted is notoriety and all you really desire leads to celebrity and where stardom is the only point of reference. What's new about this novel is how unconsciously casual the characters' drives are. This lust is as natural to them as being American-it's almost a birthright." – Bret Easton Ellis

"Daisy, Paque, and Stella want. They want to be actresses. They want to be in a band. They want to be models. They want to be famous, damn it. And so…they each tell their story of forming a girl group, moving to LA, and flirting with fame. Clarke doesn't hate his antiheroines–he just views them as by-products of the culture: glitter-eyed, vacant, and cruel. The satire works, sliding down as silvery and toxic as liquid mercury." - *Entertainment Weekly*

"Jaime Clarke is a masterful illusionist; in his deft hands, emptiness seems full, teenage pathos appears sassy and charming. *We're So Famous* is a blithe, highly entertaining indictment of the permanent state of adolescence that trademarks our culture, a made-for-TV world where innocence is hardly a virtue, ambition barely a value system." – Bob Shacochis

"Clarke seems to have created a crafty book of bubble letters to express his anger, sending off a disguised Barbie mail bomb that shows how insipid and money-drenched youth culture can be." – *Village Voice*

"Jaime Clarke's novel *We're So Famous* follows Stella, Paque, and Daisy–three utterly talentless girls from Phoenix who share a near-horrifying affinity for Bananarama. But it's only after Daisy and Paque's unwitting connection to a double murder helps skyrocket their band, Masterful Johnson, to nationwide stardom that the story really gets going. Through a string of pop-culture references (Neve Campbell, Dennis Hopper, Jennifer Grey's nose job) and mishaps (an unfortunate lip-synching tragedy a la Milli Vanilli, movie deals, smack), Clarke keeps the satire sharp and his heroines clueless." – *Spin Magazine*

"Darkly and pinkly comic, this is the story of a trio of teenage American girls and their pursuit of the three big Ms of American life: Music, Movies and Murder. An impressive debut by a talented young novelist." – Jonathan Ames

"This first novel is plastic fantastic. Daisy, Paque and Stella are talentless teens, obsessed by Bananarama and longing for stardom. They love celebrity and crave the flashbulbs and headlines for themselves. The girls become fantasy wrestlers, make a record, get parts in a going-nowhere film, then try to put on big brave smiles in the empty-hearted world of fame. Sad, sassy and salient." – *Elle Magazine*

"*We're So Famous* smartly anticipates a culture re-configured by the quest for fame. The starry-eyed girls at the center of this rock-and-roll fairy tale are the predecessors of today's selfie-snappers. With biting wit and wry humor, Clarke brilliantly reminds us that we've always lived for likes." – Mona Awad

Made in the USA
Middletown, DE
14 June 2018